MW01047969

The Mysteroius Case
of
Ebenezer Scrooge

BY
WRIGLEY BROGAN

ISBN 978-1494751746

Ink & Lens, Ltd.

To Joan Slack

Also by Wrigley Brogan:

Gecko
The Hands of Esau
Shandar @ killcongress.com

The Mysterous Case
of
Ebenezer Scrooge
by
Wrigley Brogan

=================================

The housekeeper found his body on the morning of the 25th – Christmas day. We decided to treat the death as a homicide. Scrooge was, after all, greatly disliked. Said to be the most disreputable, crotchety, and stingy bastard in the neighborhood, he had plenty of enemies. It had snowed the night before and he remained, a twisted twig frozen in the cold when, I arrived. They were about to take him away and I gave him one last look. He did not look frightened and his lips were turned up in a smile. Even his eyes glowed like a kid's with a new toy. Another impression dimpled the snow as if something had fallen there but been re-

1

moved. Too many people leaving too many footprints had clouded the scene.

The boys pried up the body and placed it on the stretcher. Scrooge's arms and legs stuck to the sides like the wings of an airplane.

Several people stood around the outline, men in coats and top hats, women in long dresses and muffs, bonnets tied tightly about their heads. I inspected the other impression dimpling the snow. Something had flattened the snow into a large bowl. I picked up a feather. The feather had fallen after the snowfall. There was no way to tell if there was a connection.

"Anyone see what happened?" I said.

"Serves him right," said a man. He tapped his cane in the snow. The other people swayed quietly. "He was a mean one, he was. Never talked to anyone except to complain. Not a kind word, I tell you."

"We all knew him," said a woman. Her muff wiggled and I imagined she was twirling her hands to keep them warm. "We didn't like him, but we knew him."

"Did you see what happened?" I said to no one in particular.

"I wouldn't say if I did," said the first man.

"That kind of talk can get you run in. Do you want to try again."

"No, I didn't see anything."

"How about the rest of you?"

"No one liked him," said a man fiddling with the buttons on his coat. I was here last night."

"Who are you?"

"Mr. Hawkins. I work with the Children's Society. Harvy and I came by the other day seeking a donation. He wasn't in so we returned last night. He did nothing except ridicule us and send us on our way. We pleaded our case sighting the Christmas spirit and told him that a great many children go hungry every day. He would hear nothing of it. He said that's the state's job, not his. I said a little extra wouldn't hurt."

I knew of Hawkins and the Children's Society. Ninety percent of everything they collected went into their pockets – administrative costs they claimed. The director dressed in the finest livery and their office made a king's palace look shabby.

"So you weren't exactly a fan of Scrooge?" I said.

"A fan? Not on your life. We're all better off with him dead. Imagine that; a man that won't give something for children on Christmas."

"Where were you this morning?"

"This morning?" Everyone looked his way. "Why, sir, I was in my abode snuggled tight as a bug."

"Can you prove it?"

"Well, of course. My wife was there. We had been to the company party last night and were quite tired when we got in."

"Lots of liquor?"

"Liquor, I resent the implication." His face reddened as he swelled more than would a man of innocence.

"Can I get in touch with you at the office?"

"I've been there for twenty years."

My hands were cold and I found it difficult to take notes with my stiff fingers. The housekeeper answered the door and seemed reluctant to let me in. Her mouth was stuffed with chocolates. The fire was raging and she sweated. Scrooge might have been tight with others, but not with the house. The furniture was the finest and paintings covered the wall including a Monet and two Turners not to mention several other old classics.

"I understand you found the body?" I said.

"Yes sir," she said.

I could hardly understand her with all the chocolates in her mouth. She seemed a little embarrassed and did not offer me a seat. The chocolates were in a silver bowl and a silver tea service sat on a custom coffee table.

"What say we talk a little? When did you find him?"

"Oh, it was early, sir. Right early. I was out to get the milk. He only takes a half -liter a week and uses it sparingly. Imagine, only a half-liter. That's enough for your tea. He was a careful man in everything except the house, that's right enough. He wouldn't have used that in a week except it would go bad."

I walked about the room taking inventory and stopped near the fireplace to thaw my hands.

"And you found him when you came back?"

"Yes sir. He was flat as could be, his head all twisted up and a silly look on his face. He was up several times in the night and went out sometime after midnight. That's strange, I thought. He never goes out. There was all kinds of rattling about in his room that kept me awake. That's how I knew he left"

"Maybe he had a woman up there." I attempted to rattle her, break up her story. I couldn't imagine him with a woman, too old, too crusty, too dried out.

"Oh, no no. He weren't that kind of man. He would have found a woman an expense even if he didn't have to out-right pay for her. They might have took him for the money later."

"Show me his room." I put my notebook back in my pocket. "Did he always keep the sitting room so hot?"

"I didn't see the harm in it," she said. "There's

5

plenty of coal and I expect I'll be on the street soon enough. He wouldn't be the kind to leave me anything so I'll have to make out the best I can."

His bedroom was on the next flight up, a large room with high and heavy doors. The window was open and the curtains flapped from a slight breeze. From the window I saw his impression in the snow. People were still gathered around. His bed was a mess, all the covers tossed up like waves in a storm. One corner of the canopy hung down and a bed curtain was torn half down.

"Some mess," I said. "There was a real struggle in here and this must be what you heard. Did you think to come up and look into the problem?"

"Oh, no, sir. He weren't the kind that wants me in here 'cept when he had a special need. Cooking, cleaning, and washing, that's my job. Sometimes he took liberties with me thinking I didn't have to be paid any extra. That's why he didn't need no woman. 'Why pay for the cow' some says. He had the cow and the milk for free and I kept my job right enough. I didn't like it none but employment's hard to come by and he weren't too demanding and if I could get away for a while I stayed out at night so's he didn't get no ideas."

6

"Did it make him angry if you were out and he wanted you?"

"If he got any special urges, and I weren't around, he played with his lizard." She sat on the bed and rolled the edge of a sheet in her hands.

"His lizard? Most men wouldn't talk about that kind of thing."

"He didn't tell anyone, but it was common knowledge with me. I seen him through the keyhole when he weren't looking. Every time it got cold and he thought I weren't around his lizard went stiff and he grabbed hold of the damn thing to warm it up. It was right strange I say. I heard about men doing such things but I never seen it before. He shook his lizard until it got warm and when the thing went limp he was happy enough, a big stupid look on his face. Reckon he was sick that way."

I decided to change the subject. Even I was getting embarrassed although she was not bothered. I suspected she was a harder woman than she let on.

"What about his business? Did he ever say much about it?"

"Nar a thing 'cept to complain about old Bob Cratchit. Said he was useless and earned mor'n he was worth. He would of fired him 'cept he couldn't get another one so cheap and he knew he couldn't get no job someplace else. Worked for a dog's wages, he did, and happy to get it. Didn't have a lick of pride and took that abuse day after day. If you ask me, Cratchit had a conniving streak and was up to something."

"How about family?"

"Cratchit, you mean?"

"No, Scrooge."

"A nephew is all," she said. As if upset, or just flushed, she dabbed at her face with the sheet. "A fine boy, Fred is, a fine boy. He didn't think the world of his uncle, but thought of him well enough. Felt sorry for him I think. Thought he was a bitter and lonely old man. He never seen his faults like the rest of us did."

"And what did Scrooge think of him?"

I looked out the window again. Although just one story up, the ground was still a long way down, especially for a frail old man.

"He didn't think nothing of him, same as he didn't think of everyone else, either."

"Do you know where he went when he went out?"

"The nephew?"

"Don't be daft," I said. "Where did Scrooge go in the middle of the night? Did he have some regular place?"

"Reckon he went to the tea shop round the corner. It's a rough place full of night people, actors and musicians and such. Women too, if you knows what I mean." She winked and fluttered her eyebrows.

I looked at his picture on the nightstand.

"Mind if I take this?"

"It means nothing to me."

I pulled the picture from the frame and walked two blocks to the Piquad. They served more than tea. They had scones, hard as cement, and dried sausages and meat pies covered with gummy gravy, and kegs of beer. If not for the tea the Piquad would have been considered a pub, and a rough one at that. The tea gave them respectability, a place trying to rise in the world. The coffee was overpriced, thick and bitter and I heard rumors that people loved it. The proprietor didn't look any too prosperous.

"I'm detective Checkers," I said. "You the owner?"

"Snudic. It's on the nametag. I'm the manager. Marge Suni owns the place. She ain't here."

"Early morning of the 25th. You working then?"

"That's Marty. He always works that shift. I think he's here taking inventory in back. You want to talk to him?"

"Sure," I said.

"You want a tea?'

"Earl Grey?"

"Sure."

He flopped a tea bag in a cup and dumped in the hot water. The water flowed yellow from the bag. He pushed the sugar and milk my way and disappeared. He returned with a tall bundle of bones in a Tee shirt and headband sprouting red hair.

"You want me?" the bundle said.

"You Marty?"

"Yeh."

"You working the morning of the 25th?"

"Yeh."

"You know a man named Scrooge?"

"Nah."

"How about this?" I removed the picture of Scrooge from my pocket. He took the picture and looked at it closely.

"Oh, him," said Marty. "He came in half out of his mind – crazy he was – scared half to death. He said he'd been seeing ghosts. Man, he was on something bad, real bad."

"Did he say what frightened him?" He handed back the picture and sat on a stool. I sipped at the tea.

"He said his old partner, some guy named Morley, came to see him."

"Do you mean Marley, Jacob Marley?"

"Maybe that was it. Marley, Morley, Mable, something like that. He gave me this big story about this guy showing up and said some ghosts or angles were going to visit him. He didn't believe him and the guy got pissed off and left and the guy in the picture figured he was just dreaming cause he ate a bad egg or something. When he went to sleep one of them came buy and dragged him all over town."

"Did he describe him, the ghost, I mean?"

"He didn't say. The ghost grabbed him by the hand and flew him out the window. I thought, wooh, stay clear of this fella. When I tried to get away he held me by the arm and said the ghost took him to the past and he saw himself as a boy. And there was some fuzzywiggle guy and a big dance and everyone was having a great time. He said there was this hot little number at the dance whose pants he wanted to get into but never did on account of he had no guts. Then he starts to cry about everything cause he screwed up his whole life so I get him a brew and he drinks the thing down in one gulp. I'm thinking about calling the cops when he says 'bah humbug', throws the glass across the room and stomps out. He never even paid for nothing. I wasn't going to go after him, not in his condition. You never know what crazy folks will do. I never saw him again. You looking for him?"

"He's dead."

"Dead – when?"

"Found him this morning outside his upper floor window."

"Maybe you ought to find this Mellow fellow."

"Marley - he's dead, too."

I went back to the neighborhood before going to see his nephew, Fred. The crowd had shrunk. Murder fades quickly in that part of town. They would return with their friends after spreading the story. Two boys stood nearby laughing.

"What you boys laughing at?" I said.

"Scrooge," said the short one with the torn coat. "Serves him right?"

"What serves him right?" I said.

"That he's dead."

I didn't tell them I was a cop. Boys in this neighborhood didn't talk to cops without repercussions from their pals.

"I wonder who killed him?"

"Could be anyone. Sometimes we knocked his hat off with a snowball and he got all pissed. Other guys laughed knowing we didn't mean nothing. Not him, not old Scrooge. He took everything personal."

"Is that all?"

"We shouldn't tell you this, mister, but he was weird."

"Weird how?" They seemed to freeze up and huddled in closer so the words would not spread. "I won't tell anyone, I promise."

"OK. You promise?" They waited for me to nod. "He tried to get us up to his room. Said he had something special for us up there."

"Did he say what it was?"

"He sure did. He said if we went up and promised not to tell anyone he would show us his lizard. He said if we were special good he might let us touch it."

"Did you ever go?"

"We ain't no perverts. We ain't touching nothing don't belong to us."

At that they ran off stopping to scoop up some snow and molding it into balls.

Fred lived at the other side of town, a little upscale block containing short strips of classy apartments, the kinds with a balcony too small to be of any use, above the door. A young woman answered the door. She could not speak English but grinned a lot.

"Is Fred Hitchins here?" She nodded "yes" then shook her head "no" then nodded "yes" again.

"I'll get it, twitzoid said a man I took to be Fred. "We brought her from Doolitzstan and she can't even wash the dishes."

"You know what they say about good help?" I said.

"It's true enough," said Fred. "Paid good

money, too. As soon as they cross the border they go to hell, have a litter of kids and live off the rest of us respectable folks. Most of the time they won't do any work. People who won't lift a finger to help themselves drive me crazy."

"I'm detective Checkers. I am sorry to say that your uncle is dead and I want to ask you a few questions."

"Sure. It was bound to happen. Come on in and I'll see if I can get that woman to get us some coffee." Fred was surprised at the death and he showed no emotion. He did not even seem curious.

"No need; I won't be here that long. What kind of relationship did you have with your uncle?"

"He was a crabby old bastard," said Fred. "I was always friendly around him because it so annoyed him. He hated anyone happy so I would give him the old Christmas cheer routine. Drove him nuts. This time every year I get a good laugh."

"I understand he had a will." I didn't know that for sure but it's always a good question to get people squirming.

"Who knows?" said Fred. "I'm pretty well set with the money my mother left me. I don't have to work a day in my life."

"That would be Fan?"

"That's her, Scrooge's sister. Sometimes I think

14

she was the only friend he had and she made me promise to treat him nice."

"Did they get along?"

"Like I said. I guess they got along well enough. She said she used to walk him home from school every day. He even mentioned it once himself."

"I understand you're getting married?"

"She's got the cash, too." His face brightened. "Her family's in the banking business and her Grandfather is Lord Lemer. They made a fortune the last time the economy went to hell. She's a good bet to keep my money safe and I guess I'll be moving up in the world. That's what comes from working hard."

"Did you notice anything strange about your uncle's behavior lately."

"He was here last night."

"Last night?"

"This morning, I guess, early, about three. I had some friends over and we stayed up late playing whist. Someone noticed a movement at the window. I went over and saw my Uncle looking through the window. He had this dazed look on his face and he seemed to be talking to someone. I knew he was a lot of things, but never a peeping Tom. When I went out to ask him in he had vanished. Took off in a big hurry, I'd say."

"And you never saw him again?"

"No. Ralph Mertleman came in with some ale not long after and said he saw him wandering all over the streets like he was looking for something. I thought about looking for him but it's mighty cold outside and I have this skin thing going on. It's like he was trying to see everything that was going on."

Cratchit was my next stop. I knew he was a dumpy little man with a gimpy kid and he seemed to be a breeder with a house full of brats. His house was in a depression of soggy walkways and soot-covered buildings of shady bricks and barred windows. Soot had blackened the snow and icicles leaked brown water. A cripple with crutches answered the door. I took him to be Tiny Tim, Cratchit's boy.

"Does Bob Cratchit live here?" I said.

"What's it to ya?" he said. He looked at me and sneered.

"Would you tell him Detective Walter Checkers wants to talk to him."

"Tell him yourself. You ain't no cripple. Did you bring me anything? Most folks bring a cripple something."

A man rounded the corner squeaking like a mouse. "Now, now," he said to the boy. "Let's be polite to the man."

"Piss off," said Tiny Tim. He farted as he left.

"I'm terribly sorry," said Cratchit. "The boy's a bit high strung. It's not easy be disabled. People pick on you and you don't get the same breaks as others. May I help you?"

"I'm detective Checkers." I flashed him my badge. "Your boss was found dead this morning. Do you know anything about it?"

"Dead. Dead. I can't believe he's dead." I thought he was going to pass out. "He was such a wonderful man." Cratchit seemed truly distressed – maybe a bit too distressed. "Please come in." He escorted me to the kitchen. "This is the warmest room. I must get Mrs. Cratchit. This is my oldest daughter, Martha. She can keep you occupied."

Cratchit scurried off and I eyed Martha - or she eyed me. She was a tall lanky thing and she lifted her leg and placed her foot on a stool. She twisted her head and, without smiling, lifted her dress and adjusted her stocking.

"You want a drink?" she said. "Coffee or tea? Maybe a little sweetener in it?"

"Whatever you have," I said.

She poured a cup of tea with cream, licked her finger and stuck it into the liquid. "It's hot," she said. "It's very hot and very sweet."

She brought the drink over slowly and placed a hand on my shoulder and leaned across my back to place the cup on the table. Her cheek carefully touched mine and she turned her lips to the edge of mine and said, "Yes, VERY hot and VERY sweet."

Cratchit returned with a two-legged dumpling wearing an apron the size of a throw rug. "This is the misses," he said. "We're terribly shook up. I can't believe anyone would hurt him."

"Who said anyone hurt him?"

"Oh, oh. I only assumed. Why else would they send a detective?"

"When did you last see Scrooge?"

"Just last night." He slapped his cheeks. "We were working late. His nephew came to wish us a Merry Christmas. A good boy, a very good boy. He brought us a brandy to celebrate. Mr. Scrooge drank much more than he should have. He liked the bottle." Cratchit placed a finger beside his nose and raised his eyebrows. "I dare say he was a bit inebriated when he left."

"Nothing else unusual?"

"No. Not at all."

"I understand he was always tight with the coal."

"A shrewd businessman, nothing more. He was not one to send money up the chimney. Any investment was safe with him and he taught me many things like moving closer to the fire if I was cold."

I decided to take a chance so I threw out my

usual question to get his reaction. "What about the will?" He started to dance about the room and twitter like a spider monkey. His wife covered her face and sobbed. "I told you, Bob; I told you. But you wouldn't listen."

"I wasn't intentional," he said. "There was no harm. I took out the policy just as a chance. Who knew that someone would kill him?"

"A chance?" I was not sure what he meant. "When did you buy the will?"

"I know it looks bad. I took out the will last week. Just a fluke, you understand. Double indemnity in case of murder."

"That's going to take some explaining."

"I loved the old man dearly, really I did. I had nothing to do with it, nothing. Some people refused to see Mr. Scrooge's good qualities and there had been threats on his life. I thought a small life insurance policy would do no harm and it was a better bet than the lottery. Go on, dear. Bring detective Checkers the policy. He'll see there's no harm in a little will."

She rolled out of the kitchen and returned a minute later with a folded envelope. She continued to cry as she handed the papers to me. I unfolded them carefully.

"Whew, that's some policy," I said. "If this is small, what do you consider large?"

"He owed me!" said Cratchit, banging his fist

on the table. His face twisted like a dried plum and spittle ran from between his lips. His voice quickly quieted. "There won't be any problem with the policy, will there?"

"I'm not an insurance man," I said. "As long as you're not involved in his death I don't see any trouble. Maybe you can get an operation to help Tiny Tim walk again."

Cratchit took back the insurance policy. "Oh him," he said. "He'll be OK."

I decided to check in with Lodge, the M.E. He always had his hands and mouth full of food. He stood eating a chicken leg over a stripped down Scrooge.

"Anything new," I said.

"Not much." He chewed around the bone of the chicken. "I found this in his pocket."

He handed me a piece of paper on Marley and Scrooge letterhead. "Is the future certain?" I thought about the paper for a minute then read the note again. "What do you make of this?" I said. Lodge shrugged his shoulders.

"Who knows about the future?" he said. "He seemed worried about what was going to happen."

"Aren't we all? Anything else?"

"Nothing," he said. "Not even a wallet. Smashed flat as a pancake and his legs were broken from the fall, including a few ribs."

"What about the tox report? Anything strange running around his system."

"It's a wonder he lasted this long," said Lodge. "His entire system was saturated with Angel Dust and soaked in alcohol. He must have been half out of his mind with such a mix. That much juice would probably have killed him within hours."

"Do you think someone killed him? I mean, is there any indication?"

"Don't ask me to do your jab," said Lodge. "Not that I can see. I looked for bruises on his back, in case he had been pushed, but didn't find any. If he was pushed he wasn't pushed hard enough to leave any marks. There were no physical signs of a struggle, no marks on his head or face. Who knows? Shoving him out the wondow would not have taken much effort."

I walked back to Scrooge's place. As I suspected, a larger crowed lingered around the impression. They were talking amongst themselves and pointing at the window. One young boy seemed reluctant and shy. Something did not look right. I pulled him to the side to question him without the others hearing.

"OK son, what's the story?"

"Nothing sir; nothing."

"I'm a cop. Do you know what can happen to you for lying to a cop? You could be in a lot of trouble." Kids lie easily, but badly. They have not learned the nuances that come with years of practice. Small ticks and expressions give them away. "Come on, what's the story."

"I wanted the money," he said. He tried to shy away. I held him back.

"What money?"

"I was just walking down the street when a crazy man started screaming from that window." He pointed to the open window in Scrooge's building.

"Who started screaming?"

"The dead man. He said to me 'boy, boy, come here.' Then he pulled out a handful of money. My mamma told me about those kinds of people trying to give a kid money. I came anyway. I had never see so much money and I thought I would be safe if I did not go in the house."

"Then what happened?"

"He asked about the giant goose round the corner. He wanted to know if it was still there. I told him I thought it was and he started to laugh and said I was a remarkable boy and he threw me a bunch of money. He said if I brought back the goose I could keep the extra money and he would give some more if I hurried. I picked up the notes and ran off. I didn't think I was doing anything wrong."

"Did you get the goose?"

"I sure did. It was even bigger than I thought. Fast as I could I could I brought it back. He was still in the window and still laughing. I never saw anyone so happy. He kept clapping his hands together and leaning back and forth and saying how remarkable I was. Then he tossed me a bunch more money. I was afraid to take it but I looked around and no one was there so I started to pick it up. Then he asked me to throw up the goose. I told him I couldn't throw that far but he told me to try anyway and when I tried the goose fell back down."

"What happened then? Did he come and get the goose?"

"He said to grab the goose by the head and swing it around. I gave it a few good swings and let it go. He started laughing and clapping as the bird flew up. It didn't go up far enough and he reached out and tumbled from of the window. I think he laughed all the way down. When he fell he didn't move. There was still no one around. I snatched the purse that was hanging from around his neck and took the bird and ran off. I didn't think no one would care."

So that was the story. Happiness and the Christmas spirit killed Scrooge. I went into the house to tell the housekeeper. People were everywhere and two men were carrying out a table. Almost everything in the house was gone.

Not a picture hung on the wall.

"Some kind of fire sale?" I said.

"Oh." She seemed surprised and a little embarrassed. "I thought I would have some of Mr. Scrooge's things put away for safekeeping. Yes, for safekeeping. I wouldn't want anything to happen to them."

"He fell out of the window," I said. "Case closed."

"Then no one killed him?" She seemed disappointed.

"Hey lady," said a man walking toward the door. "How much for the box?"

"No, not that," she said.She went toward the man. "Don't take that." She grabbed the box.

"What's with the box," I said. "Everything else is going out of here fast enough."

"I forgot to close the bedroom window. It's Scrooge's lizard, the one he always played with when I wasn't around. It froze stiff as can be." She lifted the lid. A hard blue and green lizard lay stretched inside. "What you reckon I should do with the thing?"

"Give it to me," I said. I closed the lid on the box and walked outside. The crowd had grown even larger. "What are you all doing here?" I waved my arm. "Scrooge fell out of the window, that's all. There was no murder, just an accident."

"It's Christmas," said a woman.

"So, it's Christmas," I said. "Go home and celebrate with your families. There's nothing to see here."

"Something doesn't seem right," another woman said. "It feels like we should do something. We don't want to abandoned someone on Christmas."

"Christmas, Schrimas," I said. "So, god bless you everyone. Now get the hell out of here and go home."

Made in the USA
Middletown, DE
04 February 2025